MW01006163

POE KNOWS

POE KNOWS

A MISCELLANY OF MACABRE MUSINGS

With Illustrations by Taylor Dolan

U

UNION
SQUARE
& CO.

NEW YORK

**UNION
SQUARE
& CO.**

NEW YORK

UNION SQUARE & CO. and the distinctive
Union Square & Co. logo are trademarks of
Sterling Publishing Co., Inc.

Union Square & Co., LLC, is a subsidiary of
Sterling Publishing Co., Inc.

ISBN 978-1-4549-4524-6
ISBN 978-1-4549-4635-9 (e-book)

For information about custom editions, special sales,
and premium purchases, please contact
specialsales@unionsquareandco.com.

Printed in the United States of America

2 4 6 8 10 9 7 5 3 1

unionsquareandco.com

Interior design by Kevin Ullrich
Cover design by Jo Obarowski

CONTENTS

INTRODUCTION

I've been a thinking, whether it were best
To take things seriously or all in jest

—"Oh Tempora! Oh Mores!"

Can you believe that Edgar Allan Poe, that master of the macabre and the morose, tossed off lines as flippant as these? The truth is Poe was a master of the bon mot, and all of his works—fiction, poetry, and essays—are laced with witticisms and irresistibly quotable passages. This volume collects more than 200 quotes, aphorisms, and Poesque displays of verbal virtuosity, culled from his fiction, poetry, essays, nonfiction, and letters—just about everything Poe produced. We've divided the contents into ten thematic chapters that show the range and diversity of just what Poe was a thinking.

INTRODUCTION

Of course, death and darkness predominate in Poe's writing—or at the very least in the works best known to most readers. The man had a preoccupation with premature burial that bordered on the morbid—so much so that he wrote a story under that title in which he imagined himself a character who nearly suffers the same fate as the victims of live burial he describes in the tale. Numerous quotes in this compilation suggest that Poe was not a true believer in a firmly fixed boundary between life and death, which is why characters in some of his stories speak or manifest from beyond the grave. Ask him what accentuated the beauty of a woman in a poem, and he would tell you, with a perfectly straight face, her death.

It will surprise many readers of this volume that Poe also had a wicked sense of humor. Who else but someone preoccupied with the dark side would have a character chortle gleefully about how War and Pestilence are actually beneficial to mankind, or say in praise of

Purgatory that "a man may go farther and fare worse." There's even a trace of the whimsical in the ravings of Poe's mad characters, who are so convinced of their lucidness that they give away their condition by harping on it giddily.

If the quotes compiled for this volume show anything, it is the scope of Poe's intellect and the brilliance with which he commented on everything from the character of genius to the complexity of coincidence, the speciousness of spirituality, and the perversity of human nature. It will surely astound you to discover just how much Poe knew.

BEAUTY

It is indisputable that Edgar Allan Poe appreciated beauty. References to beauty and the beautiful are omnipresent in "The Philosophy of Composition," the famous essay in which he referred to poetry as an expression of rhythmical beauty. It was in that same essay that he identified the death of a beautiful woman as the most poetic topic in the world. Most of us would think that just a tad morbid, but it certainly explains why so much of Poe's poetry and fiction features ladies and lovers on death's doorstep—or across the threshold. For Poe, death and the maiden were inextricably intertwined. What a killjoy!

I would define, in brief,
the Poetry of words as
*The Rhythmical Creation
of Beauty.*

—*The Poetic Principle*

THE DEATH . . . OF A BEAUTIFUL WOMAN IS, UNQUESTIONABLY, THE MOST POETICAL TOPIC IN THE WORLD.

— The Philosophy of Composition

That pleasure which is at once the most intense, the most elevating, and the most pure, is, I believe, found in the contemplation of the beautiful.

—*The Philosophy of Composition*

BEAUTY OF WHATEVER KIND, IN ITS SUPREME DEVELOPMENT, INVARIABLY EXCITES THE SENSITIVE SOUL TO TEARS. MELANCHOLY IS THUS THE MOST LEGITIMATE OF ALL THE POETICAL TONES.

—The Philosophy of Composition

The magic of a lovely form
in woman—the necromancy
of female gracefulness—was
always a power which I had
found it impossible to resist.

—*The Spectacles*

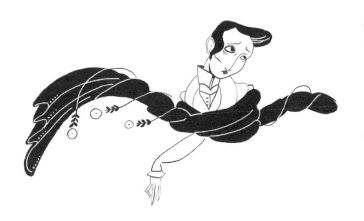

THERE IS NO EXQUISITE BEAUTY ... WITHOUT SOME *STRANGENESS* IN THE PROPORTION.

—Ligeia

When, indeed, men speak of Beauty, they mean, precisely, not a quality, as is supposed, but an effect—they refer, in short, just to that intense and pure elevation of *soul—not* of intellect, or of heart.

—*The Philosophy of Composition*

BEAUTY

TO GENIUS BEAUTY GIVES LIFE—REAPING OFTEN A REWARD IN IMMORTALITY.

—Fifty Suggestions

The *pure Imagination* chooses, from *either Beauty or Deformity,* only the most combinable things hitherto uncombined.

—*Marginalia*

Just as the Intellect concerns itself with Truth, so Taste informs us of the Beautiful while the Moral Sense is regardful of Duty.

—*The Poetic Principle*

HOW IS IT THAT FROM
BEAUTY I HAVE DERIVED
A TYPE OF UNLOVELINESS?—
FROM THE COVENANT OF
PEACE, A SIMILE OF SORROW?

—*Berenice*

DEATH

In his more metaphysical musings, Poe pondered the boundary that separates life and death, asking where the one ends and the other begins. You could say it was something of an obsession with him—as was the horror of premature burial. Yet he simply refused to acknowledge the finality of the feast of the conqueror worm. In one of his tales, a man hypnotized as he is dying continues to converse in his mesmeric fugue for days from beyond the grave. In several other stories, dead lovers return to possess their successors. In Poe's work, the dead just won't stay down.

There are two bodies—the rudimental and the complete; corresponding with the two conditions of the worm and the butterfly. What we call "death," is but the painful metamorphosis.

—*Mesmeric Revelation*

DEATH

Should you ever be drowned or hung, be sure and make a note of your sensations—they will be worth to you ten guineas a sheet.

—*How to Write a Blackwood Article*

DEATH

THE PLAY IS THE TRAGEDY, "MAN," AND ITS HERO, THE CONQUEROR WORM.

—The Conqueror Worm

EVEN IN THE GRAVE ALL IS NOT LOST.

—The Pit and the Pendulum

To die laughing must be the most glorious of all glorious deaths!

—*The Assignation*

AND THEN THERE STOLE
INTO MY FANCY, LIKE A
RICH MUSICAL NOTE, THE
THOUGHT OF WHAT SWEET
REST THERE MUST BE IN
THE GRAVE.

—The Pit and the Pendulum

DEATH

Our present incarnation is progressive, preparatory, temporary. Our future is perfected, ultimate, immortal. The ultimate life is the full design.

—*Mesmeric Revelation*

33

I SAW THAT SHE MUST DIE—AND I STRUGGLED DESPERATELY IN SPIRIT WITH THE GRIM AZRAEL.

—Ligeia

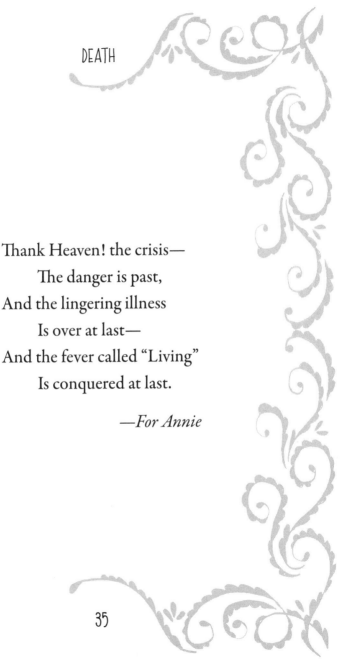

DEATH

Thank Heaven! the crisis—
The danger is past,
And the lingering illness
Is over at last—
And the fever called "Living"
Is conquered at last.

—*For Annie*

SHE CAME AND DEPARTED
AS A SHADOW.

—*Ligeia*

DEATH

I AM DYING, YET SHALL I LIVE.

—Morella

The corpse, I repeat, stirred, and
now more vigorously than before.

—*Ligeia*

Oh, outcast of all outcasts most
abandoned!—to the earth art
thou not forever dead?

—*William Wilson*

To be buried while alive is, beyond question, the most terrific of these extremes which has ever fallen to the lot of mere mortality.

—*The Premature Burial*

In me didst thou exist—and,
in my death, see by this image,
which is thine own, how utterly
thou hast murdered thyself.

—*William Wilson*

THE BOUNDARIES WHICH DIVIDE LIFE FROM DEATH ARE AT BEST SHADOWY AND VAGUE. WHO SHALL SAY WHERE THE ONE ENDS, AND WHERE THE OTHER BEGINS?

– The Premature Burial

It may be asserted, without hesitation, that *no* event is so terribly well adapted to inspire the supremeness of bodily and of mental distress, as is burial before death.

—*The Premature Burial*

Alas! the grim legion of sepulchral terrors cannot be regarded as altogether fanciful—but, like the Demons in whose company Afrasiab made his voyage down the Oxus, they must sleep, or they will devour us—they must be suffered to slumber, or we perish.

—*The Premature Burial*

DARKNESS AND DECAY
AND THE RED DEATH HELD
ILLIMITABLE DOMINION
OVER ALL.

—*The Masque of the Red Death*

EVEN WITH THE UTTERLY
LOST, TO WHOM LIFE AND
DEATH ARE EQUALLY JESTS,
THERE ARE MATTERS OF
WHICH NO JEST CAN BE MADE.

—*The Masque of the Red Death*

DEATH

There can be no more absolute waste of
time than the attempt to *prove*, at the
present day, that man, by mere exercise
of will, can so impress his fellow, as to
cast him into an abnormal condition,
of which the phenomena resemble very
closely those of *death*, or at least resemble
them more nearly than they do the
phenomena of any other normal
condition within our cognizance.

—*Mesmeric Revelation*

IN PACE REQUIESCAT!

—The Cask of Amontillado

DREAMS

Dreams are not just dreams in Poe's poetry and prose. They are sometimes idyllic captures of an idealized past or the means by which individuals glimpse eternities and truths obscured to the waking world. In Poe's work, people dream not only by night but also by day. No wonder he challenged the integrity of our waking reality by famously asking whether all that we see or seem is "but a dream within a dream." Of course nightmares are also dreams, and they also can be found in abundance in his writings. But let's not ruin the mood here.

POE KNOWS

IT IS A HAPPINESS TO WONDER;—
IT IS A HAPPINESS TO DREAM.

—Morella

DREAMS

They who dream by day are cognizant
of many things which escape those
who dream only by night. In their gray
visions they obtain glimpses of eternity,
and thrill, in awaking, to find that they
have been upon the verge of the great
secret. In snatches, they learn something
of the wisdom which is of good, and
more of the mere knowledge which
is of evil.

—Eleonora

Is *all* that we see or seem

But a dream within a dream?

—*A Dream Within a Dream*

Yet if hope has flown away

In a night, or in a day,

In a vision, or in none,

Is it therefore the less *gone?*

—*A Dream Within a Dream*

Arousing from the most profound of slumbers, we break the gossamer web of *some* dream. Yet in a second afterward, (so frail may that web have been) we remember not that we have dreamed.

—*The Pit and the Pendulum*

DREAMS

Dreams! in their vivid colouring of life—
As in that fleeting, shadowy, misty strife
Of semblance with reality which brings
To the delirious eye more lovely things
Of Paradise & Love—& all our own!

—Dreams

Ah! what is not a dream by day

To him whose eyes are cast

On things around him with a ray

Turned back upon the past?

—*A Dream*

DREAMS

By a route obscure and lonely,
Haunted by ill angels only,
Where an Eidolon, named Night,
On a black throne reigns upright,
I have reached these lands but newly
From an ultimate dim Thule—
From a wild weird clime that lieth, sublime,
    Out of Space—out of Time.

—Dream-Land

OH! THAT MY YOUNG LIFE WERE A LASTING DREAM!

—Dreams

DREAMS

THOSE WHO DREAM AS I,
ASPIRINGLY, ARE DAMNED,
AND DIE.

—*Introduction*

My hopes are dying

While, on dreams relying,

I am spelled by art.

—*To Miss Louise Olivia Hunter*

DREAMS

My draught of passion hath

    been deep—

I revell'd, and I now would sleep.

       —Introduction

Now, when one dreams, and, in the dream, suspects that he dreams, the suspicion *never fails to confirm itself*, and the sleeper is almost immediately aroused.

—*A Tale of the Ragged Mountains*

DREAMS

The realities of the world affected me
as visions, and as visions only, while the
wild ideas of the land of dreams became,
in turn, not the material of my every-day
existence, but in very deed that existence
utterly and solely in itself.

—*Berenice*

IT IS BY NO MEANS AN
IRRATIONAL FANCY THAT,
IN A FUTURE EXISTENCE,
WE SHALL LOOK UPON WHAT
WE THINK OUR PRESENT
EXISTENCE, AS A DREAM.

—*Marginalia*

EMOTION

For all his morbidness of mood and somberness of thought, Poe was an incurable romantic. His characters believe in love at first sight. They mourn the passing of youthful passion but remain love-smitten all their lives. So many of Poe's characters are persons of sentiment who revel in the intensity of their feelings, even though their excitement is beyond their rational understanding. But these emotions are often a double-edged sword for them. Hope occasionally proves a torture when it goes unfulfilled, and love is sometimes felt most acutely when it is lost. To be a feeling character in Poe's work is to be vulnerable.

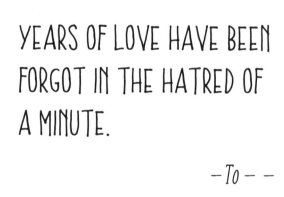

YEARS OF LOVE HAVE BEEN
FORGOT IN THE HATRED OF
A MINUTE.

—To — —

I have no words—alas!—to tell

The loveliness of loving well!

—*Tamerlane*

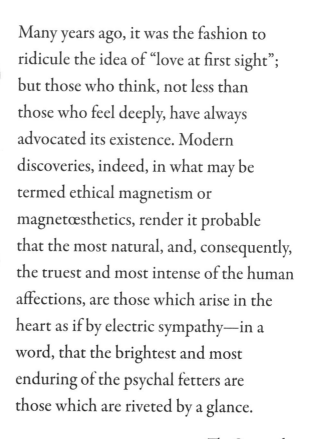

Many years ago, it was the fashion to ridicule the idea of "love at first sight"; but those who think, not less than those who feel deeply, have always advocated its existence. Modern discoveries, indeed, in what may be termed ethical magnetism or magnetœsthetics, render it probable that the most natural, and, consequently, the truest and most intense of the human affections, are those which arise in the heart as if by electric sympathy—in a word, that the brightest and most enduring of the psychal fetters are those which are riveted by a glance.

—*The Spectacles*

IN THE STRANGE ANOMALY
OF MY EXISTENCE, FEELINGS
WITH ME, *HAD NEVER BEEN*
OF THE HEART, AND MY
PASSIONS *ALWAYS WERE*
OF THE MIND.

—*Berenice*

Young Love's first

lesson is—the heart.

—*Tamerlane*

O, human love! thou spirit given,

On Earth, of all we hope in Heaven!

—Tamerlane

THERE ARE CHORDS IN THE HEARTS OF THE MOST RECKLESS WHICH CANNOT BE TOUCHED WITHOUT EMOTION.

— *The Masque of the Red Death*

A sense of insufferable gloom pervaded my spirit. I say insufferable; for the feeling was unrelieved by any of that half-pleasurable, because poetic, sentiment, with which the mind usually receives even the sternest natural images of the desolate or terrible.

—*The Fall of the House of Usher*

Never to suffer would have been
never to have been blessed.

—*Mesmeric Revelation*

I had so worked upon my imagination
as really to believe that about the whole
mansion and domain there hung an
atmosphere peculiar to themselves and
their immediate vicinity—an atmosphere
which had no affinity with the air of
heaven, but which had reeked up from
the decayed trees, and the gray wall, and
the silent tarn—a pestilent and mystic
vapor, dull, sluggish, faintly discernible,
and leaden-hued.

—*The Fall of the House of Usher*

While, beyond doubt, there *are* combinations of very simple natural objects which have the power of thus affecting us, still the analysis of this power lies among considerations beyond our depth.

—*The Fall of the House of Usher*

I love, indeed, to regard the dark valleys,
and the grey rocks, and the waters that
silently smile, and the forests that sigh in
uneasy slumbers, and the proud watchful
mountains that look down upon all—
I love to regard these as themselves but
the colossal members of one vast animate
and sentient whole.

—*The Island of the Fay*

PASSION MUST, WITH YOUTH, EXPIRE.

— Tamerlane

HUMAN NATURE

Poe was an astute student of human nature. He made an avatar of the human impulse to do the wrong thing even when its wrongness is recognized and named it "the imp of the perverse." He identified "diddling," or the swindling of others, as a uniquely human endeavor worthy of anatomizing in a story so titled. Poe extemporized on both the best and the worst of human nature, but it was the latter in particular that engaged his fancy and inspired some of his most acerbic observations on mankind's mercurialness.

NEAR NEIGHBORS ARE SELDOM FRIENDS.

—Metzengerstein

The desire to be well must be excited simultaneously with any principle which shall be merely a modification of combativeness, but in the case of that something which I term *perverseness*, the desire to be well is not only not aroused, but a strongly antagonistical sentiment exists.

—*The Imp of the Perverse*

I am not more certain that I breathe,
than that the assurance of the wrong
or error of any action is often the
one unconquerable *force* which
impels us, and alone impels us to
its prosecution.

—*The Imp of the Perverse*

IN THE MANNER OF THE TRUE
GENTLEMAN, WE ARE ALWAYS
AWARE OF A DIFFERENCE FROM
THE BEARING OF THE VULGAR,
WITHOUT BEING AT ONCE
PRECISELY ABLE TO DETERMINE
IN WHAT SUCH DIFFERENCE
CONSISTS.

—*The Assignation*

Many persons, I considered, are prone to estimate commodities in their possession—however valueless to the then proprietor—however troublesome, or distressing—in direct ratio with the advantages to be derived by others from their attainment, or by themselves from their abandonment.

—*Loss of Breath*

There are some secrets which do not permit themselves to be told. Men die nightly in their beds, wringing the hands of ghostly confessors, and looking them piteously in the eyes—die with despair of heart and convulsion of throat, on account of the hideousness of mysteries which will not *suffer themselves* to be revealed.

—*The Man of the Crowd*

A wrong is unredressed when retribution overtakes its redresser. It is equally unredressed when the avenger fails to make himself felt as such to him who has done the wrong.

—*The Cask of Amontillado*

The singularity of this coincidence absolutely stupified me for a time. This is the usual effect of such coincidences. The mind struggles to establish a connexion—a sequence of cause and effect— and, being unable to do so, suffers a species of temporary paralysis.

—*The Gold-Bug*

We should bear in mind that, in general, it is the object of our newspapers rather to create a sensation—to make a point— than to further the cause of truth. The latter end is only pursued when it seems coincident with the former. The print which merely falls in with ordinary opinion (however well founded this opinion may be) earns for itself no credit with the mob. The mass of the people regard as profound only him who suggests *pungent contradictions* of the general idea.

—*The Mystery of Marie Rogêt*

Diddling—or the abstract idea conveyed by the verb to diddle—is sufficiently well understood. Yet the fact, the deed, the thing *diddling*, is somewhat difficult to define. We may get, however, at a tolerably distinct conception of the matter in hand, by defining—not the thing, diddling, in itself—but man, as an animal that diddles.

—Diddling Considered as One
of the Exact Sciences

The spirit of PERVERSENESS. Of this spirit philosophy takes no account. Yet I am not more sure that my soul lives, than I am that perverseness is one of the primitive impulses of the human heart— one of the indivisible primary faculties, or sentiments, which give direction to the character of Man.

—*The Black Cat*

MOST WRITERS—POETS IN
ESPECIAL—PREFER HAVING
IT UNDERSTOOD THAT THEY
COMPOSE BY A SPECIES OF
FINE FRENZY.

—The Philosophy of Composition

MEN USUALLY GROW BASE
BY DEGREES. FROM ME, IN AN
INSTANT, ALL VIRTUE DROPPED
BODILY AS A MANTLE.

—*William Wilson*

Whenever a rich old hunks, or prodigal heir, or bankrupt corporation, gets into the notion of putting up a palace, there is no such thing in the world as stopping either of them, and this every intelligent person knows.

—*The Business Man*

The world is made up of all kinds of persons, with all modes of thought, and all sorts of conventional customs.

—*The System of Doctor Tarr and Professor Fether*

There is something in the unselfish and self-sacrificing love of a brute, which goes directly to the heart of him who has had frequent occasion to test the paltry friendship and gossamer fidelity of mere *Man*.

—*The Black Cat*

The reign of manners hath long ceased,
For men have none at all, or bad at least.

—*Oh Tempora! Oh Mores!*

BLACK CATS ARE ALL OF THEM WITCHES.

—Instinct vs. Reason—A Black Cat

POE KNOWS

CATS ARE MODEST.

—Desultory Notes on Cats

Merely to breathe was enjoyment;
and I derived positive pleasure
even from many of the legitimate
sources of pain. I felt a calm but
inquisitive interest in every thing.

—*The Man of the Crowd*

He was too much a man of the world either to laugh like the dog, or by shrieks to betray the indecorous trepidation of the cat.

—*Bon-Bon*

Diddling, rightly considered, is a compound, of which the ingredients are minuteness, interest, perseverance, ingenuity, audacity, *nonchalance*, originality, impertinence, and *grin*.

—*Diddling Considered as One of the Exact Sciences*

Upon mankind at large the events of very early existence rarely leave in mature age any definite impression.

—*William Wilson*

I dare say you have often observed
this disposition to temporize, or to
procrastinate, in people who are
laboring under any very poignant
sorrow. Their powers of mind seem
to be rendered torpid, so that they
have a horror of anything like action,
and like nothing in the world so well
as to lie quietly in bed and "nurse their
grief," as the old ladies express it—that
is to say, ruminate over their trouble.

—*"Thou Art the Man"*

A deficiency of imagination has been imputed to me.

—MS. *Found in a Bottle*

Man is an animal that diddles, and there is *no* animal that diddles *but* man.

—*Diddling Considered as One of the Exact Sciences*

THE TEEMING BRAIN OF
CHILDHOOD REQUIRES
NO EXTERNAL WORLD
OF INCIDENT TO OCCUPY
OR AMUSE IT.

—William Wilson

What disease is like Alcohol!

—*The Black Cat*

THERE IS NO PASSION IN NATURE SO DEMONIACALLY IMPATIENT, AS THAT OF HIM, WHO SHUDDERING UPON THE EDGE OF A PRECIPICE, THUS MEDITATES A PLUNGE.

—The Imp of the Perverse

A thousand vague fancies oppressed and disconcerted me—fancies the more distressing because vague.

—*A Tale of the Ragged Mountains*

What can be more soothing, at once to a man's Pride and to his Conscience, than the conviction that, in taking vengeance on his enemies for injustice done him, he has simply to do them *justice* in return?

—*Marginalia*

As far as I can understand the "loving our enemies," it implies the hating our friends.

—*Fifty Suggestions*

I'VE BEEN A THINKING,
WHETHER IT WERE BEST
TO TAKE THINGS SERIOUSLY
OR ALL IN JEST.

—*Oh Tempora! Oh Mores!*

Who has not, a hundred times, found himself committing a vile or a silly action, for no other reason than because he knows he should *not?* Have we not a perpetual inclination, in the teeth of our best judgment, to violate that which is *Law*, merely because we understand it to be such?

—*The Black Cat*

IT IS A TRAIT IN THE PERVERSITY OF HUMAN NATURE TO REJECT THE OBVIOUS AND THE READY, FOR THE FAR-DISTANT AND EQUIVOCAL.

—Loss of Breath

HORROR

Of course Poe had incisive things to say about horror. Horror is not only an emotional response felt by characters in his works, it is an essential element of the experiences they endure. In his elaborate allegorical poem "The Conqueror Worm," Poe likened the drama of life to "a play of hopes and fears" driven by "much of Madness, and more of Sin, /And Horror the soul of the plot." His characters often are plunged into horror when they least expect it, or when they are enjoying their greatest pleasure. Small wonder that he could say of its inescapable ubiquity, "horror and fatality have been stalking abroad in all ages."

Things may be imagined, but
words have no power to impress
the mind with the exquisite
horror of their reality.

—*The Narrative of Arthur Gordon
Pym of Nantucket*

NOW AND THEN, ALAS, THE CONSCIENCE OF MAN TAKES UP A BURTHEN SO HEAVY IN HORROR THAT IT CAN BE THROWN DOWN ONLY INTO THE GRAVE. AND THUS THE ESSENCE OF ALL CRIME IS UNDIVULGED.

–The Man of the Crowd

HORROR AND FATALITY HAVE BEEN STALKING ABROAD IN ALL AGES.

—*Metzengerstein*

126

There are certain themes of which the interest is all-absorbing, but which are too entirely horrible for the purposes of legitimate fiction. These the mere romanticist must eschew, if he do not wish to offend, or to disgust. They are with propriety handled, only when the severity and majesty of truth sanctify and sustain them.

—*The Premature Burial*

In the phrases and expressions of the dead on the lips of the loved and the living, I found food for consuming thought and horror—for a worm that *would* not die.

—*Morella*

To conceive the horror of
my sensations is, I presume,
utterly impossible; yet a
curiosity to penetrate the
mysteries of these awful regions,
predominates even over my
despair, and will reconcile me
to the most hideous aspect
of death.

—MS. *Found in a Bottle*

Deep into that darkness peering, long I
stood there wondering, fearing,
Doubting, dreaming dreams no mortal
ever dared to dream before.

—*The Raven*

JOY SUDDENLY FADED INTO HORROR, AND THE MOST BEAUTIFUL BECAME THE MOST HIDEOUS.

—Morella

IT WAS NO WONDER THAT HIS CONDITION TERRIFIED—THAT IT INFECTED ME. I FELT CREEPING UPON ME, BY SLOW YET CERTAIN DEGREES, THE WILD INFLUENCES OF HIS OWN FANTASTIC YET IMPRESSIVE SUPERSTITIONS.

—The Fall of the House of Usher

To the substances of terror
he was sufficiently alive, but
of its shadows he had no
apprehension.

—*The Sphinx*

Have I not indeed been living in a dream? And am I not now dying a victim to the horror and the mystery of the wildest of all sublunary visions?

—*William Wilson*

Desolate yet all undaunted, on this

desert land enchanted—

On this home by Horror haunted.

—*The Raven*

TERROR IS NOT OF GERMANY, BUT OF THE SOUL.

—Preface, Tales of the Grotesque and Arabesque

TO AN ANOMALOUS SPECIES OF TERROR I FOUND HIM A BOUNDEN SLAVE.

—The Fall of the House of Usher

I HAVE, INDEED, NO ABHORRENCE OF DANGER, EXCEPT IN ITS ABSOLUTE EFFECT—IN TERROR.

—The Fall of the House of Usher

MADNESS

The madmen in Poe's work are among his most interesting characters, in no small part because they are convinced they are not mad. The narrator of "The Tell-Tale Heart" has rationalized his madness as a noble sensitivity, if only to himself. Indeed, it is often hard to tell Poe characters who are merely emotionally overwrought from those who are genuinely unhinged. In "The System of Doctor Tarr and Professor Fether," the narrator is not aware that the lunatics have taken over the asylum he is visiting, so logically do they express themselves. Madness is not only hard to spot in a Poe character, it is sometimes hard to argue with.

The question is not yet settled, whether madness is or is not the loftiest intelligence—whether much that is glorious—whether all that is profound—does not spring from disease of thought— *moods* of mind exalted at the expense of the general intellect.

—*Eleonora*

MADNESS

YOU FANCY ME MAD.
MADMEN KNOW NOTHING.

—The Tell-Tale Heart

WHAT YOU MISTAKE FOR
MADNESS IS BUT OVER
ACUTENESS OF THE SENSES.

—The Tell-Tale Heart

A lunatic may be "soothed," as it is called, for a time, but, in the end, he is very apt to become obstreperous. His cunning, too, is proverbial, and great. If he has a project in view, he conceals his design with a marvellous wisdom; and the dexterity with which he counterfeits sanity, presents, to the metaphysician, one of the most singular problems in the study of mind. When a madman appears *thoroughly* sane, indeed, it is high time to put him in a straight jacket.

—*The System of Doctor Tarr and Professor Fether*

There were times, indeed, when
I thought his unceasingly agitated
mind was laboring with some oppressive
secret, to divulge which he struggled
for the necessary courage. At times,
again, I was obliged to resolve all into
the mere inexplicable vagaries of madness.

—*The Fall of the House of Usher*

TO REPOSE CONFIDENCE IN THE UNDERSTANDING OR DISCRETION OF A MADMAN, IS TO GAIN HIM BODY AND SOUL.

— The System of Doctor Tarr and Professor Fether

Why *will* you say that I am mad?
The disease had sharpened my
senses—not destroyed—not
dulled them.

—*The Tell-Tale Heart*

There is no argument which so touches the feeble reason of the madman as the *reductio ad absurdum.*

—*The System of Doctor Tarr and Professor Fether*

MADNESS IS NO COMFORTABLE FEELING.

—*Hop-Frog*

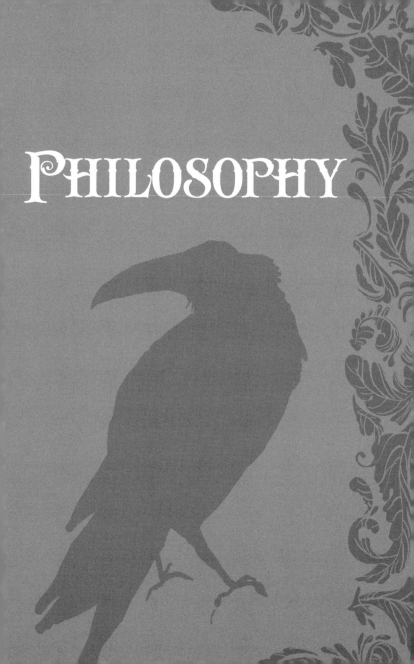

PHILOSOPHY

Philosophical thought is a thread woven into the fabric of many of Poe's works. At its very simplest it is evident in the thoughts of his narrators, who spend a considerable amount of time attempting to articulate their reasoning for their behavior. The majority of Poe's work, fiction as well as nonfiction, is laced with philosophical asides and insights. He expressed theories on everything from the proper unity of impression for storytelling to the way coincidence shapes our belief in the supernatural. Who else but Poe would write "Eureka," a 40,000-word philosophical treatise on the cosmography of the universe, and subtitle it "A Prose Poem."

The poetic sentiment implies an abnormally keen appreciation of poetic excellence, with an unconscious assimilation of it into the poetic entity, so that an admired passage, being forgotten and afterwards reviving through an exceedingly shadowy train of association, is supposed by the plagiarising poet to be really the coinage of his own brain.

—*Marginalia*

PROVIDED THE MORALS OF AN AUTHOR ARE PURE, PERSONALLY, IT SIGNIFIES NOTHING WHAT ARE THE MORALS OF HIS BOOKS.

—Never Bet the Devil Your Head

If any literary work is too long to be read at one sitting, we must be content to dispense with the immensely important effect derivable from unity of impression.

—*The Philosophy of Composition*

In my own heart there dwells no faith in
præter-nature. That Nature and its God
are two, no man who thinks, will deny.
That the latter, creating the former, can,
at will, control or modify it, is also
unquestionable. I say "at will"; for the
question is of will, and not, as the insanity
of logic has assumed, of power. It is not
that the Deity *cannot* modify his laws,
but that we insult him in imagining a
possible necessity for modification. In
their origin these laws were fashioned to
embrace *all* contingencies which *could*
lie in the Future. With God all is *Now*.

—*The Mystery of Marie Rogêt*

Experience has shown, and a true philosophy will always show, that a vast, perhaps the larger portion of truth, arises from the seemingly irrelevant. It is through the spirit of this principle, if not precisely through its letter, that modern science has resolved to *calculate upon the unforeseen.*

—*The Mystery of Marie Rogêt*

I could now find room to doubt the evidence of my senses; and seldom called up the subject at all but with wonder at the extent of human credulity, and a smile at the vivid force of the imagination.

—*William Wilson*

WORDS ARE VAGUE THINGS.

— *The Colloquy of Monos and Una*

WORDS—PRINTED ONES
ESPECIALLY—ARE
MURDEROUS THINGS.

— *Marginalia*

In reading some books we occupy ourselves chiefly with the thoughts of the author; in perusing others, exclusively with our own.

—*Marginalia*

Every fiction *should have* a moral; and, what is more to the purpose, the critics have discovered that every fiction *has*.

—*Never Bet the Devil Your Head*

POETRY AND TRUTH ARE ONE.

—Eureka

It is folly to assert, as some at present are fond of asserting, that the Literature of any nation or age was ever injured by plain speaking on the part of the Critics.

—*Marginalia*

The most notorious ill-fortune
must, in the end, yield to
the untiring courage of
philosophy.

—*Loss of Breath*

THERE ARE MOMENTS WHEN, EVEN TO THE SOBER EYE OF REASON, THE WORLD OF OUR SAD HUMANITY MUST ASSUME THE ASPECT OF HELL.

—Marginalia

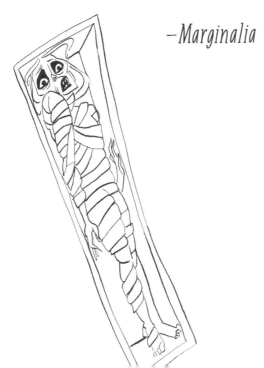

I MAKE NO EXCEPTION,
EVEN IN DANTE'S FAVOR:—
THE ONLY THING WELL
SAID OF PURGATORY,
IS THAT A MAN MAY GO
FARTHER AND FARE WORSE.

—Marginalia

A strong argument for the religion of Christ is this—that offenses against *Charity* are about the only ones which men on their death-beds can be made—not to understand— but to *feel*—as *crime.*

—*Marginalia*

There are few persons, even among the calmest thinkers, who have not occasionally been startled into a vague yet thrilling half-credence in the supernatural, by *coincidences* of so seemingly marvelous a character that, as *mere* coincidences, the intellect has been unable to receive them.

—*The Mystery of Marie Rogêt*

WE MUST NEGLECT OUR
MODELS AND STUDY
OUR CAPABILITIES.

—Marginalia

If we cannot comprehend God
in his visible works, how then in his
inconceivable thoughts, that call
the works into being? If we cannot
understand him in his objective
creatures, how then in his substantive
moods and phases of creation?

—*The Imp of the Perverse*

Pure Diabolism is but Absolute Insanity. Lucifer was merely unfortunate in having been created without brains.

—*Marginalia*

I have no belief in spirituality.
I think the word a *mere* word.
No one has really a conception
of spirit. We cannot imagine
what is not.

—*Letter to James Russell Lowell*

BY PERSON WE
UNDERSTAND AN
INTELLIGENT ESSENCE
HAVING REASON.

—Morella

IS IT NOT A LAW
THAT NEED HAS A
TENDENCY TO ENGENDER
THE THING NEEDED?

—Marginalia

No nation upon the face of the earth has ever acknowledged more than *one god*.

—*Some Words with a Mummy*

THE GREATER AMOUNT
OF TRUTH IS IMPULSIVELY
UTTERED; THUS THE
GREATER AMOUNT IS
SPOKEN, NOT WRITTEN.

—*Marginalia*

THE WISE ARE WISELY AVERSE FROM DISBELIEF.

—Marginalia

All things are either good or bad by comparison. A sufficient analysis will show that pleasure, in all cases, is but the contrast of pain. *Positive* pleasure is a mere idea. To be happy at any one point we must have suffered at the same.

—*Mesmeric Revelation*

IN GENERAL, OUR FIRST
IMPRESSIONS ARE THE
TRUE ONES.

—Marginalia

There are few cases in which mere popularity should be considered a proper test of merit.

—*Marginalia*

The nose of a mob is its imagination.
By this, at any time, it can be quietly led.

—*Marginalia*

184

PHILOSOPHY

In looking at the world *as it is*,
we shall find it folly to deny that,
to worldly success, a surer path
is Villainy than Virtue.

—*Marginalia*

This monomania, if I must so term it, consisted in a morbid irritability of those properties of the mind in metaphysical science termed the *attentive*.

—*Berenice*

SO STRICTLY COMPARATIVE IS EITHER GOOD OR ILL.

— The Narrative of Arthur Gordon Pym of Nantucket

An infinity of error makes its way into our Philosophy, through Man's habit of considering himself a citizen of a world solely—of an individual planet—instead of at least occasionally contemplating his position as cosmopolite proper—as a denizen of the universe.

—*Marginalia*

It is no longer philosophical to base,
upon what has been, a vision of what is
to be. *Accident is* admitted as a portion
of the substructure. We make chance a
matter of absolute calculation. We subject
the unlooked for and unimagined, to the
mathematical *formulae* of the schools.

—*The Mystery of Marie Rogêt*

I am above the weakness of
seeking to establish a sequence
of cause and effect, between
the disaster and the atrocity.

—*The Black Cat*

I AM OVERBURTHENED
WITH THE MAJESTY OF ALL
THINGS—OF THE UNKNOWN
NOW KNOWN—OF THE
SPECULATIVE FUTURE
MERGED IN THE AUGUST
AND CERTAIN PRESENT.

*—The Conversation of Eiros
and Charmion*

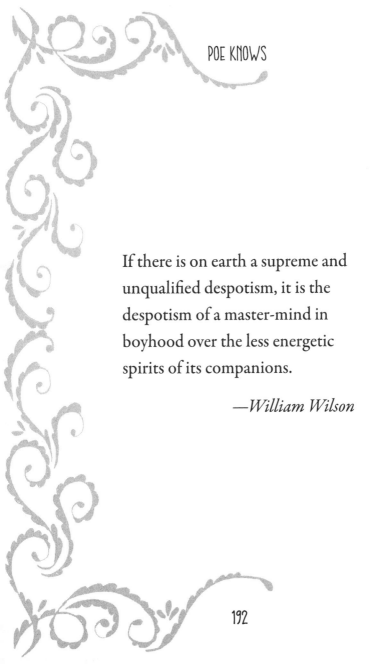

If there is on earth a supreme and unqualified despotism, it is the despotism of a master-mind in boyhood over the less energetic spirits of its companions.

—*William Wilson*

OH, GIGANTIC PARADOX, TOO UTTERLY MONSTROUS FOR SOLUTION!

—William Wilson

The mental features discoursed of as the analytical, are, in themselves, but little susceptible of analysis. We appreciate them only in their effects. We know of them, among other things, that they are always to their possessor, when inordinately possessed, a source of the liveliest enjoyment.

—*The Murders in the Rue Morgue*

As the strong man exults in his physical
ability, delighting in such exercises as
call his muscles into action, so glories
the analyst in that moral activity
which *disentangles*. He derives pleasure
from even the most trivial occupations
bringing his talent into play. He is
fond of enigmas, of conundrums, of
hieroglyphics; exhibiting in his solutions
of each a degree of *acumen* which
appears to the ordinary apprehension
præternatural. His results, brought about
by the very soul and essence of method,
have, in truth, the whole air of intuition.

—*The Murders in the Rue Morgue*

Where breathes the man who has traversed, and successfully, *all* the wide areas of moral, physical, and mathematical science?

—*Ligeia*

The faculty of re-solution is possibly much invigorated by mathematical study, and especially by that highest branch of it which, unjustly, and merely on account of its retrograde operations, has been called, as if *par excellence*, analysis. Yet to calculate is not in itself to analyse.

—*The Murders in the Rue Morgue*

I dread the events of the future, not in themselves, but in their results.

—*The Fall of the House of Usher*

True method appertains to the ordinary and the obvious alone, and cannot be applied to the *outré*.

—*The Business Man*

YOUR MIND WAVERS, AND ITS AGITATION WILL FIND RELIEF IN THE EXERCISE OF SIMPLE MEMORIES. LOOK NOT AROUND, NOR FORWARD—BUT BACK.

— *The Conversation of Eiros and Charmion*

Between ingenuity and the analytic
ability there exists a difference far greater,
indeed, than that between the fancy and
the imagination, but of a character very
strictly analogous. It will be found, in fact,
that the ingenious are always fanciful,
and the *truly* imaginative never otherwise
than analytic.

—*The Murders in the Rue Morgue*

I am a business man. I am a
methodical man. Method
is *the* thing, after all.

—*The Business Man*

The analytical power should
not be confounded with simple
ingenuity; for while the analyst
is necessarily ingenious, the
ingenious man is often remarkably
incapable of analysis.

—*The Murders in the Rue Morgue*

The history of human knowledge has so uninterruptedly shown that to collateral, or incidental, or accidental events we are indebted for the most numerous and most valuable discoveries, that it has at length become necessary, in any prospective view of improvement, to make not only large, but the largest allowances for inventions that shall arise by chance, and quite out of the range of ordinary expectation.

—*The Mystery of Marie Rogêt*

WHAT THE WORLD CALLS "GENIUS" IS THE STATE OF MENTAL DISEASE ARISING FROM THE UNDUE PREDOMINANCE OF SOME ONE OF THE FACULTIES.

—Fifty Suggestions

The true genius shudders at incompleteness—imperfection—and usually prefers silence to saying the something which is not every thing that should be said.

—*Marginalia*

There are few persons who have not, at some period of their lives, amused themselves in retracing the steps by which particular conclusions of their own minds have been attained.

—*The Murders in the Rue Morgue*

Coincidences, in general, are great stumbling-blocks in the way of that class of thinkers who have been educated to know nothing of the theory of probabilities—that theory to which the most glorious objects of human research are indebted for the most glorious of illustration.

—The Murders in the Rue Morgue

I dispute the availability, and thus the value, of that reason which is cultivated in any especial form other than the abstractly logical. I dispute, in particular, the reason educed by mathematical study. The mathematics are the science of form and quantity; mathematical reasoning is merely logic applied to observation upon form and quantity.

—*The Purloined Letter*

Ah, not in knowledge is happiness, but in the acquisition of knowledge! In for ever knowing, we are for ever blessed; but to know all, were the curse of a fiend.

—*The Power of Words*

A strong relish for physical philosophy has, I fear, tinctured my mind with a very common error of this age—I mean the habit of referring occurrences, even the least susceptible of such reference, to the principles of that science.

—*MS. Found in a Bottle*

IN BIOGRAPHY THE TRUTH
IS EVERYTHING, AND IN
AUTO-BIOGRAPHY IT IS
ESPECIALLY SO.

—The Business Man

Science! true daughter of Old Time
     thou art!
Who alterest all things with thy
     peering eyes.
Why preyest thou thus upon the
     poet's heart,
Vulture, whose wings are dull realities?

          —Sonnet—To Science

He is the corporate Silence: dread him not!
    No power hath he of evil in himself;
But should some urgent fate (untimely lot!)
    Bring thee to meet his shadow
        (nameless elf,
That haunteth the lone regions where
        hath trod
No foot of man,) commend thyself to God!

—Sonnet—Silence

PHILOSOPHY

There are some qualities — some
     incorporate things,
    That have a double life, which thus
     is made
A type of that twin entity which springs
    From matter and light, evinced in
     solid and shade.

        —Sonnet—Silence

No thinking being lives who,
at some luminous point of his
life of thought, has not felt
himself lost amid the surges of
futile efforts at understanding
or believing that anything
exists *greater than his own soul.*

—*Eureka*

THAT THE GHASTLY
EXTREMES OF AGONY ARE
ENDURED BY MAN THE UNIT,
AND NEVER BY MAN THE
MASS—FOR THIS LET US
THANK A MERCIFUL GOD!

—*The Premature Burial*

What we feel to be *Fancy* will
be found fanciful still, whatever
be the theme which engages it.

—*Fifty Suggestions*

IF THERE IS ANY THING ON
EARTH I HATE, IT IS A GENIUS.
YOUR GENIUSES ARE ALL
ARRANT ASSES—THE GREATER
THE GENIUS THE GREATER
THE ASS.

— *The Business Man*

MEN OF GENIUS ARE FAR MORE
ABUNDANT THAN IS SUPPOSED.

—Marginalia

The great variety of melodious expression which is given out from the keys of a piano, might be made, in proper hands, the basis of an excellent fairy-tale.

—*A Chapter of Suggestions*

I will not be sure that men at present think more profoundly than half a century ago, but beyond question they think with more rapidity, with more skill, with more tact, with more of method and less of excrescence in the thought.

—Marginalia

"Ignorance is bliss"—but, that
the bliss be real, the ignorance
must be so profound as not to
suspect itself ignorant.

—*Fifty Suggestions*

Is it not truly remarkable that, before
the magnificent light shed upon
philosophy by Humanity, the world
was accustomed to regard War and
Pestilence as calamities? Do you know
that prayers were actually offered up
in the ancient temples to the end that
these *evils* (!) might not be visited
upon mankind? Is it not really difficult
to comprehend upon what principle of
interest our forefathers acted? Were
they so blind as not to perceive that the
destruction of a myriad of individuals
is only so much positive advantage to
the mass!

—*Mellonta Tauta*

THE HIGHER ORDER OF MUSIC
IS THE MOST THOROUGHLY
ESTIMATED WHEN WE ARE
EXCLUSIVELY ALONE.

– The Island of the Fay

NO THOUGHT CAN PERISH,
SO NO ACT IS WITHOUT
INFINITE RESULT.

—The Power of Words

Motion is the action of *mind*—
not of *thinking*.

—*Mesmeric Revelation*

I *cannot* conceive Infinity, and am convinced that no human being can.

—*Eureka: A Prose Poem*

THE FINEST QUALITY OF THOUGHT IS ITS SELF-COGNIZANCE.

—Eureka: A Prose Poem

Ours is a world of words:

Quiet we call

"Silence"—which is the merest

word of all.

—*Al Aaraaf*

I have no faith in human perfectibility. I think that human exertion will have no appreciable effect upon humanity.

—*Letter to James Russell Lowell*

THE CORRUPTION OF TASTE IS A PORTION OR A PENDANT OF THE DOLLAR-MANUFACTURE.

—The Philosophy of Furniture

SOLITUDE

Solitude is a recurring theme in Poe's poetry and prose, and not always as a positive state of mind. Certainly, Poe extolled the virtues of solitude for indulging in serious thought and contemplation. But more often in Poe's work solitude is a synonym for the loneliness of those who have lost loved ones, much as Poe himself experienced in his personal life with the early deaths of his mother and his young wife. Poe also knew the loneliness of those who feel they are outsiders to their time and place. "From childhood's hour I have not been / As others were" may be the most poignant line in all of Poe's writing.

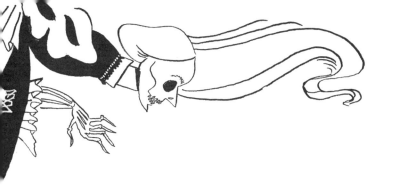

FROM CHILDHOOD'S HOUR
        I HAVE NOT BEEN
AS OTHERS WERE—I HAVE NOT SEEN
AS OTHERS SAW

—*Alone*

POE KNOWS

DEEP IN EARTH MY LOVE IS LYING AND I MUST WEEP ALONE.

–[Deep in Earth]

In the few furrows upon his cheek I read the fables of sorrow, and weariness, and disgust with mankind, and a longing after solitude.

—*Silence—A Fable*

In spring of youth it was my lot
To haunt of the wide earth a spot
The which I could not love the less—
So lovely was the loneliness
Of a wild lake, with black rock bound,
And the tall pines that towered around.

–The Lake—To – –

Thy soul shall find itself alone

'Mid dark thoughts of the gray

tomb-stone.

—*Spirits of the Dead*

How often we forget all time,
when lone
Admiring Nature's universal
throne;
Her woods—her wilds—her
mountains—the intense
Reply of HERS to OUR
intelligence!

—[Stanzas]

WE EXISTED WITHIN OURSELVES ALONE.

—The Murders in the Rue Morgue

LEAVE MY LONELINESS UNBROKEN!

—The Raven

SORROW

It would be an understatement to say that sorrow is a dominant mood in Poe's work. His characters are melancholic by nature, and their moroseness is invariably tied to the loss of a loved one. Poe considered melancholy to be "the most legitimate of all the poetical tones." In the last poem published in his lifetime, "Annabel Lee," Poe's bereft narrator lies down nightly beside the buried body of his entombed wife. His most famous poem, "The Raven," is a paean to the pathological melancholy of a man who labors to find "surcease of sorrow" over his lost lover, only to encounter its repeated refutation. Nevermore, indeed.

Either the memory of past bliss is the anguish of to-day, or the agonies which *are*, have their origin in the ecstacies which *might have been*.

—*Berenice*

MISERY IS MANIFOLD.
THE WRETCHEDNESS OF
EARTH IS MULTIFORM.

—*Berenice*

The happiest day—the happiest hour
    My sear'd and blighted heart
        hath known,
The highest hope of pride, and power,
    I feel hath flown.

—*[The Happiest Day]*

I felt that I breathed an atmosphere of sorrow. An air of stern, deep, and irredeemable gloom hung over and pervaded all.

—*The Fall of the House of Usher*

Thy days shall be days of sorrow—that sorrow which is the most lasting of impressions, as the cypress is the most enduring of trees.

—*Morella*

SORROW

Partial oblivion is usually brought about by sudden transition, whether from joy to sorrow or from sorrow to joy—the degree of forgetfulness being proportioned to the degree of difference in the exchange.

—*The Narrative of Arthur Gordon Pym of Nantucket*

To be *thoroughly* conversant with Man's heart, is to take our final lesson in the iron-clasped volume of Despair.

—*Marginalia*

Evil is a consequence of good,
so, in fact, out of joy is sorrow
born.

—Berenice

The eye, like a shattered mirror, multiplies the images of its sorrow, and sees in innumerable far off places, the wo which is close at hand.

—*The Assignation*

QUOTH THE RAVEN "NEVERMORE."

– The Raven

About the Author

Edgar Allan Poe is universally recognized as one of the most influential writers of macabre fiction and poetry. He is credited with popularizing the tale of psychological horror and with "inventing" the detective story.

About the Illustrator

Taylor Dolan is an artist based in Arkansas with a Masters in Children's Book Illustration from the Cambridge School of Art. Her work includes an illustrated edition of *The Phantom of the Opera* and the *Ghost Scouts* series for young readers.